For Bex, Protector of Oceans, with love.
– T.M.

For my little mermaids Sophia and Beaux
and merboys Piers and Oscar.
– E.W.

To my dear husband, Leo, my best friend
and greatest support.
– P.F.

First American Edition 2021
Kane Miller, A Division of EDC Publishing
Original English language edition first published by Penguin Books Ltd,
20 Vauxhall Bridge Road, London, SW1V 2SA, UK
Copyright © Penguin Books Ltd, 2019

For information contact:
Kane Miller, A Division of EDC Publishing
P.O. Box 470663
Tulsa, OK 74147-0663
www.kanemiller.com
www.usbornebooksandmore.com

Library of Congress Control Number: 2020936960

Printed in China
2 3 4 5 6 7 8 9 10

ISBN: 978-1-68464-150-5

Tamara Macfarlane ✦ Ellie Wharton

My SECRET WORLD OF Mermaids

Illustrated by
Paula Franco

Kane Miller
A DIVISION OF EDC PUBLISHING

The Secret Society
Of Mythical Creatures

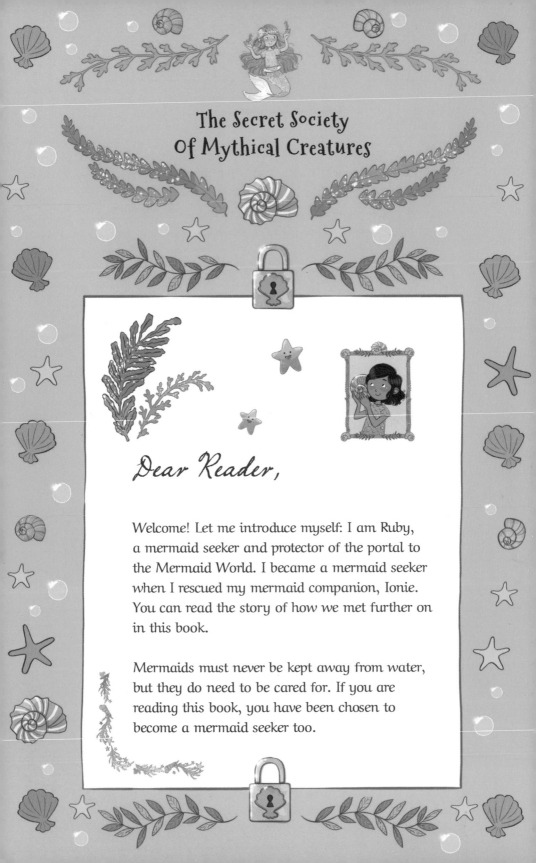

Dear Reader,

Welcome! Let me introduce myself: I am Ruby,
a mermaid seeker and protector of the portal to
the Mermaid World. I became a mermaid seeker
when I rescued my mermaid companion, Ionie.
You can read the story of how we met further on
in this book.

Mermaids must never be kept away from water,
but they do need to be cared for. If you are
reading this book, you have been chosen to
become a mermaid seeker too.

There are merfolk living in each body of water on the planet. They work hard trying to protect the oceans from human damage and destruction. I've made lots of merfriends in the waters around my home. Now it's your turn to meet these magical merfolk.

Only children who believe in magic can enter the merfolk's secret world and learn to be a mermaid seeker. This book will show you how. Have fun, but remember to keep the Mermaid World a secret.

Wishing you bubbles of joy on your journey,

Ruby

Mermaid Seeker

Secret Society of Mythical Creatures (SSMC)

Please follow any safety instructions as shown, and ask a grown-up to help you when you make food for your mermaid.

This is Ionie, my mermaid companion.

Ionie lives in the waters around my home in Australia.
She guards the portal to the Mermaid World deep at the
bottom of the ocean, and protects the colorful reefs of
the planet.

Together, we love to explore the coral reefs, coves and bays
that Ionie protects. From time to time I like to make her
favorite food – underwater jelly – and we love to play a
game of seashell bowling!

HOW TO MAKE FRIENDS WITH A MERMAID

Merfolk love children and trust them completely. This often gets them into trouble. If you follow these clues, you may just meet a mermaid. If you do, please take care of your new friend, who is counting on you.

Look out for:

⭐ A glimmer of light under the water

☆ Bubbles rising to the surface

☆ Mer-hair moving near the edges of rivers and streams (river merfolk often sleep near riverbanks and hide in the reeds)

⭐ Ripples on the water's surface

Merfolk love to play with children in their watery homes. If you look carefully beneath the surface of the water, you may glimpse one swimming below. Merfolk will say hello to any boy or girl who is kind and curious and has a sense of adventure. Could that be you?

Oh, and don't forget some seaweed sandwiches – merfolk can't resist them!

IMAGINE, INVENT, CREATE

MEET YOUR MERMAID

Let's meet your very own mermaid companion. Find your birth month and read the name of your mermaid!

If your birthday is in November, your mermaid companion is called Star Splash. If your birthday is in April, your mermaid companion is Fin Flair.

THE MONTH YOU WERE BORN:

January   Shimmer Stream
February   Aqua Ocean
March   Glitter Reef
April   Fin Flair
May   Majestic Murmur
June   Summer Spray
July   Sparkle Song
August   Glimmer Breeze
September   Seaweed Shine
October   Dewdrop
November   Star Splash
December   Tempest Tentacle

SEEKER SECRETS

When a merbaby name is being chosen, shoals of fish come to kiss the baby on the head and the bubbles from the kisses spell out the new name.

DRAW YOURSELF MEETING YOUR MERMAID COMPANION

What would your very own mermaid look like? Draw them here, using these questions to help you with your picture.

Where will you meet? It could be near the cold waters of the Arctic or in the warm seas of the Indian Ocean.

What color is their tail fin? Their hair? What secret skill will they have?

What do you see under the water? Shipwrecks, starfish, seahorses or sharks, perhaps?

What sort of special pet does your mermaid have?

Mermaid **Protector** of Coral Reefs

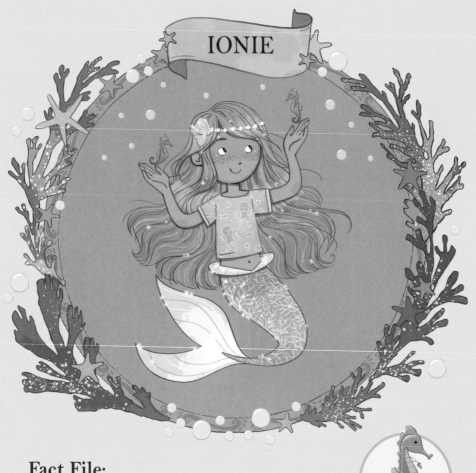

IONIE

Fact File:

Water type: Coral reefs

Place: Australia

Scale pattern: Crystal coral

Pet: Long-snouted seahorse

Favorite food: Underwater jelly

Secret skill: Can repair a coral reef with her hair

Mermaid Protector of Tide Pools

Fact File:

Water type: Tide pools

Place: British Isles

Scale pattern: Shimmering stars

Pet: Starfish

Favorite food: Tide pool pizza

Secret skill: Can write messages in the stars to communicate with other magical creatures

Mermaid Protector of Lagoons

MOON

Fact File:

Water type: Lagoons

Place: Venice, Italy

Scale pattern: Mystical moons

Pet: Short-eared owl

Favorite food: Oyster-shell cookies

Secret skill: Tail flashes like a lighthouse to guide ships across the lagoon around the city of Venice

Merboy **Protector** of Rapids

ONA

Fact File:

Water type: Rapids

Place: North America

Scale pattern: Precious palm leaves

Pet: Beaver

Favorite food: Rainbow rice

Secret skill: Can use his tail fin as a scoop to collect river flora to create a dam

Merboy Protector of Hot Springs

ECHO

Fact File:

Water type: Hot springs

Place: Japan

Scale pattern: Whimsical waterfalls

Pet: Snow monkey

Favorite food: Seaweed twists

Secret skill: Can hear the calls of sailors lost at sea

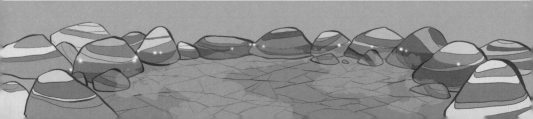

Merboy **Protector** of Oceans

OSHI

Fact File:

Water type: Oceans

Place: India

Scale pattern: Rippling waves

Pet: Killer whale

Favorite food: Seaweed sandwiches

Secret skill: Can guide killer whales to their breeding grounds through stormy seas

Mermaid **Protector** of Rivers

SHELL

Fact File:

Water type: Rivers

Place: South America

Scale pattern: Sparkling shells

Pet: Pink river dolphin

Favorite food: Starfish fortune cookies

Secret skill: Can build natural filters to help
clean the river water and protect river creatures

Merboy **Protector** of Polar Ice Caps

BLUE

Fact File:

Water type: Arctic Ocean

Place: North Pole

Scale pattern: Glistening icebergs

Pet: Narwhal

Favorite food: Glitter ice pops

Secret skill: Can blow bubbles that form an extra layer to keep warm in icy cold water

Mermaid Protector of Lakes

TALLULAH

Fact File:

Water type: Great Lakes

Place: Africa

Scale pattern: Sunny stripes

Pet: Blue heron

Favorite food: Lake lemonade

Secret skill: Can talk to birds that visit the lakes and pass on messages to land animals

Merboy Protector of Fjords

SONNI

Fact File:

Water type: Fjords

Place: Norway

Scale pattern: Vibrant ferns

Pet: River otter

Favorite food: Mermaid moss smoothies

Secret skill: Can heal whales, dolphins and otters using his tail fin

Mermaid Protector of Waterfalls

MAYA

Fact File:

Water type: Waterfalls

Place: Iguazu Falls, Argentina

Scale pattern: Tumbling rainbows

Pet: Howler monkey

Favorite food: Sea-foam floats (that's an
ice cream float to people)

Secret skill: Can send coded bubble messages to other
merfolk when an animal is in danger

Merboy **Protector** of Mountain Streams

TASHI

Fact File:

Water type: Mountain streams

Place: New Zealand

Scale pattern: Towering mountains

Pet: Mountain goat

Favorite food: Fruit scones

Secret skill: Has a superstrong tail fin so he can swim easily upstream and through waterfalls

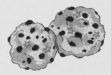

The Story
of
Ruby

The sun shone on the ocean as I dug my feet
into the sand and watched my classmates race
toward the tide pools. I was sitting looking out
at the waves, but I didn't dare go in.

If I had been back at my old school on the other side
of the world, I would have been running across the beach
with my friends. My heart ached for my old home.

As I gazed across the blue, I put a nearby shell to my ear.
I listened to the sweetest song I'd ever heard . . .

Can you hear this mermaid's song?
Listen now, it won't take long . . .

Look out yonder, turn your gaze
To find the strongest, swiftest wave.

Ride this wave, and in the end
You will find your mermaid friend.

As the song finished, a hand grasped mine. Suddenly I felt a tug and I toppled into the waves. Water swirled up around me, but as the bubbles cleared I realized that I was underwater and that a girl was holding my hand. She looked a bit like me, but had blue and pink hair, and instead of legs she had a glitter-blue tail.

I gasped! *She must be a mermaid!* I thought.

"I am Ionie," she sang. "Welcome to my home." I tried to wriggle out of her grasp, but she wouldn't let go. "You can breathe underwater while I hold your hand. Please don't be afraid. You looked so lonely on the shore – I'd like you to come and play with me and my seahorse, Snout."

The sea did look inviting, and I did feel safe with Ionie. Plus, I couldn't help but smile as Snout somersaulted around. I nodded, my heart pounding with excitement.

Ionie laughed as she led me
deeper and deeper, past coral gardens where fish
flitted like butterflies between the branches, and slow-moving
turtles meandered past me. It was like an underwater fairground!
We swam so fast in and out of coves that I felt like I was a mermaid too!

It was the most fun I'd had since moving to Australia. I
couldn't wait to swim with Ionie again. But one day, as I
waded out to a rock to meet her, Snout was there with a shell
in his mouth. Puzzled, I put it up to my ear . . .

Ruby, I need your help. Come quickly, please!
Find as much courage as you can seize.

Dive down deep, be brave, don't fret,
and release me from this silly net!

"Is Ionie in trouble?" I asked Snout. He snorted and I jumped into the water. There wasn't a moment to lose! I held my breath and dived down to the seabed, where I saw that my mermaid friend was tangled in a fishing net. I grabbed her hand so that I could breathe, and wondered how I could help her.

I need something sharp, I thought, looking around. I dived down into the murky depths and found a razor-sharp piece of coral. Then I shot straight back up and took hold of Ionie's hand again. It was hard work, but at last I set Ionie free.

The next day, when I reached our rock once more, I saw another beautiful shell. I lifted it up to my ear to listen again . . .

Dear Ruby,

Thanks for listening to my song –
It's clear you are my chosen one!
The one who saved me, bold and brave,
From perishing beneath the waves.

You have a special role to play –
A mermaid seeker, if you may.

Tonight, let's meet beneath the moon:
I'll take you to our Secret Lagoon.
Under this, in rainbow sand,
I'll lead you to Mer-Wonderland.

With love,
Ionie

MERMAID PROTECTOR
OF CORAL REEFS

My brave actions had protected a treasured mermaid and I had become a mermaid seeker! That night, as I was shown Ionie's magical home, I promised to protect it and its merfolk forever.

COLOR
ME

IMAGINE, INVENT, CREATE

CARING FOR YOUR MERMAID

Mermaids are protectors of all sea creatures, but it's
a big job and the mermaids need looking after too.
As a mermaid seeker, there are lots of things you can do.

⭐ Recycle your plastic so it doesn't end up in the sea. The
mermaids get very tired of cleaning up all the human garbage.

⭐ Mermaids love to hear new songs — it makes them very happy.
Sing songs into shells for the mermaids to hear.

⭐ Write messages in the sand. Your words will be washed out to sea for the mermaids to read.

⭐ Coral are underwater trees. The mermaids need coral to breathe. Help the mermaids by protecting the coral in any way you can.

⭐ A seashell necklace is a rare and precious thing for all merfolk. If you give one to a mermaid, it will always keep them safe. Place it in a tide pool for them to find.

ACTIVITY
Did you know that you can swim like a mermaid? We call the mermaid swimming stroke the butterfly! Try it!

MAKE, BAKE, DECORATE

SEAWEED SANDWICHES

Mermaids love seaweed. They'd eat it all day long if they could!
Here's how to make some tasty seaweed sandwiches
for your mermaid companion.

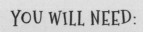

YOU WILL NEED:

1 container of
   cream cheese

2 slices of bread

1 cucumber

A grater

A knife

(Ask a grown-up to
help you use the
knife and grater.)

So healthy!

Don't forget to
make some sandwiches for
yourself. Being a mermaid
seeker is hungry work.

INSTRUCTIONS:

1

With a knife, spread some cream cheese on one slice of bread (ask a grown-up for help with this).

Yum, yum, yum!

2

Ask a grown-up to grate the cucumber into strips to look like seaweed.

3

Put the cucumber strips on top of the cream cheese.

4

Place the other slice of bread on top then cut your sandwich into triangles and serve.

The Story
of
Lara

It was a dark and stormy night. Lara pulled her hood up as she walked down to the bay. The moon hid behind thunderous clouds as she followed the sound that had lured her out of the cabin. The music drew her closer and closer to the sea.

As she reached the misty water, Lara sighed with longing. *Will I ever get to explore beneath the waves?* she wondered. Lara's parents hated the sea and she was forbidden to go near it. But the music was calling her toward the rocks at the water's edge.

At first, Lara thought that her eyes were playing tricks
on her. She hardly dared to believe it . . . It was a mermaid!

And then the mermaid sang, and her words were
crystal clear . . .

I am stuck far from home,
I am lost and all alone.

I am chilled to the very bone
On this rock all on my own.

I have no legs and cannot climb
A rock that's swathed in dirt and slime.

Help me slip beneath the waves –
Please have courage and be brave.

Lara thought quickly. The mermaid was too big to lift, and she had a tail so she couldn't climb, but perhaps her tail could help her slide back into the water . . .

"That's it!" cried Lara. "We need to make a slide."

She looked around. Shells weren't slippery and sand wasn't slippery. Just then, Lara took a step and slipped on the wet rock.

"Seaweed!" she said, laughing and pulling up handfuls from under her feet.

Lara laid a seaweed path that snaked up to the mermaid, and tucked the final strand under the mermaid's tail. Carefully, the mermaid wriggled onto the seaweed slide, and . . .

Whoosh!

Safe at last, the mermaid smiled at Lara.

"My name is Star," she sang. "Thank you for saving me, Lara. How can I ever repay your kindness?"

Lara looked at the sea and whispered her greatest wish. "Could I swim with you?" she asked, quietly hoping her wish might come true at last.

Before Lara could take another breath, she found herself deep under the water, with Star holding tightly on to her hand. Together, they swam with whales, past shimmering jellyfish and bobbing octopuses. For hours they explored beneath the sea by the light of the moon. It was more magical than Lara could ever have imagined. When they reached the shore again, the two friends promised to meet the following night.

The next morning, Lara woke and pulled a piece of seaweed out of her hair. *It wasn't a dream after all*, she thought. Running straight to the rock, she found a beautiful shell.

Lara lifted it up to her ear…

Dear Lara,

> *You are a secret mermaid keeper,*
> *A special, chosen one.*
> *Your intelligence is what we need*
> *To join the mermaid fun.*

> *Please meet me under a midnight moon*
> *And I will show you the Secret Lagoon.*
> *Under this, in jewel-colored sand,*
> *Is a portal to Mer-Wonderland.*

With love,
Star
MERMAID PROTECTOR OF TIDE POOLS

And so Lara's kindness and quick thinking meant that she would join Ruby beneath the waves. Another mermaid seeker had been found.

COLOR
ME

MERMAID MISCHIEF

Mermaids are curious and inquisitive - it's what often gets them into trouble! Here are some of their favorite things to do.

⭐ Looking after wounded fish

⭐ Playing in a seaweed maze

⭐ Watching children play on the beach

⭐ Sunbathing on the sand (without being seen!)

⭐ Exploring shipwrecks and collecting treasure

⭐ Painting murals in the sand for children to find

Dancing through the waves with dolphins!

WRITE YOUR OWN MERMAID STORY

Tell a tale of your own mermaid companion getting into trouble. What did they do? How did you protect them? Have you any tips for fellow seekers to help them keep their merfolk companions out of mischief?

MER-PETS

The merfolk always have a special pet by their side.
Mermaids need their pets to help them talk to other
magical creatures in the sea and on land. Here are some
clues to help you find a mermaid pet!

⭐ At birth, each mermaid is given a special pet by the Mer-Queen.

⭐ If the mermaid's pet is a land animal,
she will leave messages in shells
for her pet to find.

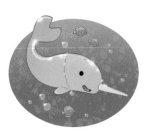

⭐ A mermaid's pet wears a tiny seashell
around its neck, held in place by a
strand of mermaid hair.

⭐ A mermaid's pet will leave
a shimmering trail of shells
wherever it goes, so that
its friend can find it.

DRAW YOUR OWN MERMAID PET AND GIVE IT A NAME. WHY IS THIS MER-PET SO SPECIAL?

SEEKER SECRETS
Mermaids use sand to polish their scales so that they are super smooth for faster swimming.

MAKE, BAKE, DECORATE

SEA-FOAM FLOATS

Mermaids love to throw a sea-foam party!
With these sea-foam floats,
you can too!

YOU WILL NEED:

A pitcher
1 bottle of a clear fizzy drink
3 drops of blue food coloring
Some vanilla ice cream
Some paper straws
A glass

1

Pour the drink into a pitcher.

2

Stir in 3 drops of blue food coloring (or enough to turn it the right shade of blue).

3

Half fill a glass with ocean drink.

4

Add a scoop of vanilla ice cream - it will foam when it mixes with the drink, creating a sea-foam float!

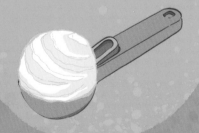

The Story
of
Jai

Jai dived under the warm water. The waves were the perfect color – a deep blue-green – and so crystal clear that he could see all the fish swimming beneath him for what seemed like miles. This was the best vacation of his life!

Kicking hard to propel himself down to the seabed, Jai noticed some brightly colored fish that he hadn't seen before. As he got nearer, the fish dashed away from him. Jai chased after them.

Suddenly he felt a hand take his and found that he could breathe underwater! A boy of about his own age was urgently beckoning him to follow. Jai gasped in surprise, and then his eyes widened further when he saw the boy's shimmering fish tail.

"Hello, I'm Oshi," said the merboy. "We need your help. Please come quickly!"

Oshi led Jai to an old shipwreck that had snapped in half on the ocean floor. It looked a little eerie inside . . .

"My friend is trapped in there!" said Oshi.

It was very dark inside the shipwreck, where the sun from
the surface only crept in through the cracks, but Jai could
hear sounds of a struggle. Through the darkness, he could
make out another merboy, trapped under the ship's boom.
Oshi let go of Jai's hand and swam over to try
to raise the boom, but it was too heavy.

Just then, Jai had an idea! *If I put my feet on the deck and push up,
I might be able to move that boom,* he thought. He pushed with all
his might, and finally the merboy was able to slip out.

Together, the three boys swam back to the shore, where they promised to meet for one last watery adventure before Jai went back to the city.

Jai smiled. "What an amazing day!"

The next morning, as Jai walked back along the beach to his grandma's hut, he saw a beautiful shell twinkling in the sunlight. He put it to his ear and listened to his friend's song:

Dear Jai,

You are a secret mermaid keeper,
A special, chosen one.
Yesterday's deep-sea adventure
Saved a precious one.

Please meet us here at noon
And we'll show you our Secret Lagoon.
Under this, in jewel-colored sand,
Is a portal to Mer-Wonderland.

With love,
Oshi
MERBOY PROTECTOR OF OCEANS

MOON CROWNS

Merfolk wear special moon crowns to a beautiful ceremony that takes place at each full moon. The merfolk gather in the Secret Lagoon for a spectacular show and to give crowns to those who have helped sea creatures. A mermaid moon crown is full of magic and power.

Can you make a moon crown for your mermaid companion? Draw your design here. You could use cardboard, tissue paper, tinfoil, flower petals, candy wrappers, glitter glue or paint.

MAKE, BAKE, DECORATE

SEAWEED TWISTS

If your mermaid companion fancies something savory, try these tasty seaweed twists.

Ask a grown-up to help you with this recipe!

YOU WILL NEED:

Some flour
1 sheet of frozen puff pastry (defrosted at room temperature)
A handful of baby spinach
½ cup of grated Parmesan
A cutting board
A rolling pin
A baking sheet and parchment paper
A knife

INSTRUCTIONS:

1 Preheat the oven to 400 degrees and line the baking sheet with parchment paper.

2 Sprinkle the cutting board with flour and lay the pastry on top of the flour. Roll it out with the rolling pin until it is about as thick as one of your fingers.

3 With the help of a grown-up, cut the pastry into strips that are about two fingers wide.

4 Lay some spinach on one of the strips and then sprinkle with Parmesan.

5 Place another strip on top, hold the ends and twist.

6 Place the twist on the baking sheet and do the same with the remaining strips.

7 Ask a grown-up to put the baking sheet in the preheated oven and bake for 10 minutes, or until the twists are golden brown.

8 Ask a grown-up to take the twists out of the oven, and try not to eat them until they have cooled down!

MAKE, SHAKE, DECORATE

SEA SMOOTHIE SURPRISE!

The mermaid seekers are getting ready for their meeting at the Secret Lagoon tonight. Tashi is making this sea smoothie surprise. Can you help him?

Ask a grown-up to help you with chopping.

YOU WILL NEED:

1 banana
2 heaped tablespoons of plain yogurt
1/2 cup of milk
A handful of spinach
1 teaspoon of honey
4 strawberries
2 tablespoons of blueberries
1 tablespoon of rolled oats
A knife
A bowl

INSTRUCTIONS:

1

Ask a grown-up to cut the end off the banana (with the skin still on) about a third of the way down. Put this to one side.

2

Peel the rest of the banana and put it with half the berries and the yogurt, milk, spinach and honey into a blender and mix until smooth.

Never use a handheld blender and always ask a grown-up for help.

3

Pour the smoothie mix into a bowl, and lay the rest of the strawberries and blueberries along one edge: these are the rocks lining the shore.

4

Sprinkle a line of oats between the smoothie sea and the rocks to make the sea foam.

5

Place the remaining end of the banana in the middle of the smoothie sea.

6

With a pen, add an eye on each side to turn the end of the banana into a fish's head popping up out of the waves.

The Story
of
Como

As Ruby, Lara and Jai met their merfolk companions at exactly the same time across the world's oceans, ready to explore Mer-Wonderland, a little boy called Como shivered in the icy Arctic weather. Outside his hut, he dropped his line through the fishing hole in the ice and sent a silent prayer into the water for food.

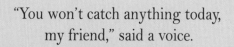

"You won't catch anything today,
my friend," said a voice.

Como smiled at his mermaid companion.
"I should've known it was because of you that
I'm hungry, Blue. Where is everyone?
What's going on?" he asked.

"A seeker meeting. Come on!" sang Blue.

And, with that, Blue pulled Como into the cool water, just as he had done
so many times before. Holding hands, they swam to the Secret Lagoon
and climbed out onto the rainbow-colored sand. The sand began to swirl
around them until a large tunnel appeared – a tunnel Como knew well. It
led straight into Mer-Wonderland.

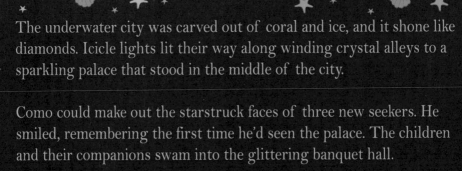

The underwater city was carved out of coral and ice, and it shone like diamonds. Icicle lights lit their way along winding crystal alleys to a sparkling palace that stood in the middle of the city.

Como could make out the starstruck faces of three new seekers. He smiled, remembering the first time he'd seen the palace. The children and their companions swam into the glittering banquet hall.

Coral chandeliers hung from the high ceilings, and the walls were studded with shiny shells. The decorations twisted up turrets and across balconies. Before them, sitting on a crystal throne, was the Mer-Queen.

Ruby, Jai, Lara and Como had not even had a chance to ask one another's names when four emperor penguins led everyone to an ice table laden with seaweed sandwiches, sea smoothie surprises, glitter ice pops and seaweed twists. A mermaid feast! The children tucked in eagerly.

Before long the show began – there was a parade of polar bears, a waltz of walruses, a diving show of dolphins and a symphony sung by seahorses. The children stared wide-eyed and clapped until their hands hurt.

As the show came to an end, the Mer-Queen swam forward gracefully. In her hands were four moon crowns. As she reached the children, they found they could breathe on their own.

"Ruby, you have been chosen to be a secret mermaid seeker because of your courage.

"Lara, you have been chosen to be a secret mermaid seeker because of your quick thinking.

"Jai, you have been chosen to be a secret mermaid seeker because of your sense of adventure.

"Finally, Como," the Mer-Queen said, "you are not a stranger to our lagoon, but no one here knows of your kindness. Even though you often go hungry, you happily share your food with the polar animals you call your friends. You protect the icy Arctic and all its creatures. Thank you."

All the merfolk clapped and cheered as the children put on their special moon crowns and, together, read an oath to protect the merfolk and all creatures of the sea. In return, the new mermaid seekers would always find friendship beneath Earth's rippling waves.

COLOR
ME

A MERMAID SONG

Mermaids have the gift of song. Write a song for your mermaid.
Think of some watery words, such as glisten, wave, splash
and shore. Then think of some mermaid words,
such as friends, magic, seashells and tails.

MAKE UP YOUR OWN SONG TO THE TUNE OF YOUR FAVORITE NURSERY RHYME.

she wos dom
popo Butt
Butt popo
Butt Buty popo

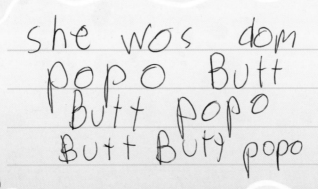

RUBY HAS WRITTEN HERS TO "ROCK-A-BYE BABY."

Magical mermaid, deep in the sea,
Glisten and shimmer only for me.
When you're in trouble, I'll hear your call.
I will protect you, I won't let you fall.

SEEKER SECRETS
A mermaid's song is the most
beautiful sound in the world.

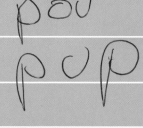

EXPLORE, INSPIRE, PROTEST

HOW MANY WAYS CAN YOU HELP MERFOLK PROTECT SEA CREATURES?

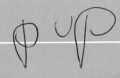

IMAGINE, INVENT, CREATE

A MERMAID TIDE POOL

Mermaids love to spend time in cooling tide pools
on rocky coastlines. Can you make a glistening tide pool
for your mermaid companion?

YOU WILL NEED:

1 sheet of tinfoil
A tray and a cup of water
Some stones and pebbles
Moss, twigs, petals and fallen leaves
1 piece of cardboard and scissors
Some colored pencils

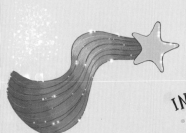

INSTRUCTIONS:

1

Place the tinfoil on the tray, then fold up the edges to make a bowl shape.

2

Arrange your stones and pebbles around the bowl to keep the foil tide pool in place.

3

Then add your moss, leaves, twigs and petals and a cup of water.

4

Draw a picture of your mermaid companion on a piece of cardboard. Cut it out and add it to your tide pool.

WRITE YOUR OWN
MERMAID SEEKER STORY

Imagine that you are swimming in the water
and a mermaid or merboy reaches out for your hand.
They need your help. What will you do next?

A final note from Ruby

Well done for completing this book.
You are now a **mermaid seeker**
and a new member of
the **Secret Society of Mythical Creatures.**

Remember to look for tiny shells left on the
sand – a mermaid might have a message for you.
Always be ready for your next watery adventure!

Keep an eye out for portals to other secret worlds too.
There are many more mythical creatures to seek!

With shimmering thanks,

Ruby

CONGRATULATIONS!

.... is a mermaid seeker.

I became a mermaid seeker
and a new member of the SSMC on ....

My mermaid companion is ....

I pledge to be kind,
be bold, be brave,
and always believe in magic.